SAY HELLO!

linda davick

beach lane books

new york • london • toronto • sydney • new delhi

SAY
HELLO!

It's lots of fun.
And here are ways
it can be done.

With a hug.

With a shake.

With a curtsy.

With a cake.

With a whisper.

With a kiss.

With a dance of happiness!

With a letter in the mail.

UNCLE WALLY
127 SEA LION DRIVE
PACIFICA, CA   94044

MAIL

With a nose.

Or with a tail.

With a smile.

With a giggle.

With a treat.

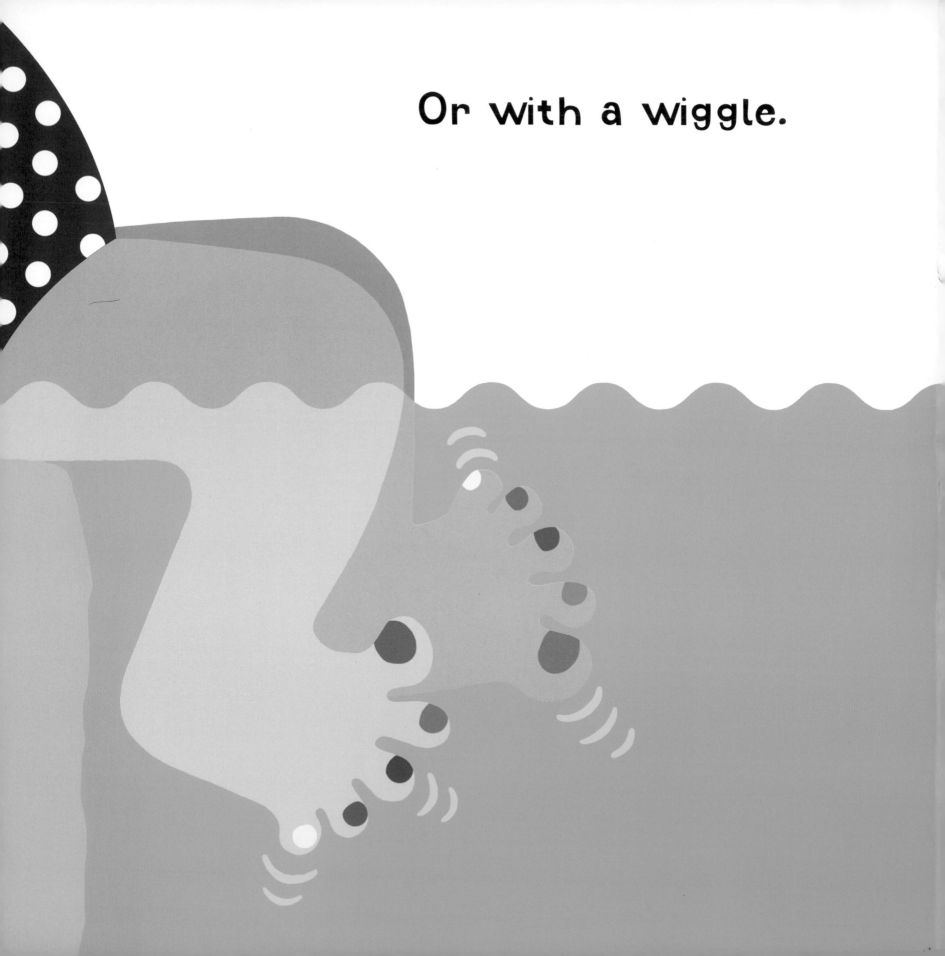

Or with a wiggle.

Don't let the moment slip away . . .

Make someone's day!

For Lucille,
the biggest HELLOer I know

BEACH LANE BOOKS • An imprint of Simon & Schuster Children's Publishing Division • 1230 Avenue of the Americas, New York, New York 10020 • Copyright © 2015 by Linda Davick • All rights reserved, including the right of reproduction in whole or in part in any form. • BEACH LANE BOOKS is a trademark of Simon & Schuster, Inc. • For information about special discounts for bulk purchases, please contact Simon & Schuster Special Sales at 1-866-506-1949 or business@simonandschuster.com. • The Simon & Schuster Speakers Bureau can bring authors to your live event. For more information or to book an event, contact the Simon & Schuster Speakers Bureau at 1-866-248-3049 or visit our website at www.simonspeakers.com. • Book design by Lauren Rille • The text for this book is set in Blocky Fill. • The illustrations for this book are rendered digitally. • Manufactured in China • 0515 SCP • First Edition • 10 9 8 7 6 5 4 3 2 1 • Library of Congress Cataloging-in-Publication Data • Davick, Linda, author, illustrator. • Say hello! / Linda Davick. — First edition. • pages cm • Summary: Illustrations and rhyming text reveal that "hello" can be said many ways, from a handshake to a dance of happiness, and that the world would be a lot more fun if more hellos were shared. • ISBN 978-1-4814-2867-5 (hardcover) — ISBN 978-1-4814-2868-2 (ebook) [1. Stories in rhyme. 2. Salutations—Fiction.] I. Title. • PZ8.3.D2658Say 2015 • [E]—dc23 • 2014014700